Darling the Curly Tailed Reindoe

Written by Cheryl Campbell

Illustrated by Steve McGinnis

Published in the United States by BQB Publishing
(Boutique of Quality Books Publishing)
www.bqbpublishing.com

Printed in the United States of America
ISBN 978-0-9828689-3-5 (h)
ISBN 978-1-939371-16-4 (p)
ISBN 978-1-937084-02-8 (e)

Library of Congress Number: 2010912312

Book and cover design
by Darlene Swanson
www.van-garde.com

In memory of Uncle Jim for his inspiration.

Darling didn't have antlers like her father, uncles, and brothers who were reindeer or even like her mother and the other reindoes. She was still too young. But Darling did have beautiful big eyes and long lashes that swept down her cheeks.

She also had a very
special tail. The other little
reindoes had tails that were just
like all the other reindeer and reindoes
in their little village at the North Pole. But
Darling's tail was different . . . it had a curl.

3

At first she didn't like her tail because it wasn't like everyone else's. As Darling grew from a pretty baby reindoe to a beautiful young reindoe, her very special curly tail grew as well.

But Darling was unhappy. She just wanted to be like all the other reindoes with short, stubby tails. She began to feel very, very sad.

Then one day Uncle Don, her favorite uncle, noticed that Darling was not playing with the other reindoes because they teased her about her tail. Suddenly, he had a great idea.

"Darling should have a cute little pail that could swing by its handle from the curl in her tail."

Darling's dad and mom, who knew that Uncle Don was wise in these matters, excitedly said, "That's it! A cute little pail to swing from the curl in her tail. What a wonderful idea!"

So Uncle Don took Darling to the workshop where the elves made toys for children all around the world. He asked them to make a pail for Darling's tail.

The elves got busy working and soon Darling
had a wonderful pail that hung from her
curly tail. She didn't feel sad any more.

Darling loved her new pail. She strutted and pranced as it hung from her tail.

Then she decided she needed something to carry in it. So the elves started sending messages to each other, the reindeer and even Santa and Mrs. Claus. Darling became very, very busy.

MAIL

One day Mrs. Claus filled Darling's pail with treats for the elves and reindeer. Soon Darling became well-known around the North Pole for her willingness to help.

With her beautiful curly tail and her wonderful pail, Darling helped out all around the North Pole. She carried messages, treats, and even hot soup when someone wasn't feeling well.

When her uncles were strengthening their sleigh-pulling skills for the big trip on Christmas Eve, Darling brought them water in the pail that was swinging from her tail.

Her uncles liked having the pail of water nearby when they became thirsty from all their sleigh pulling practice.

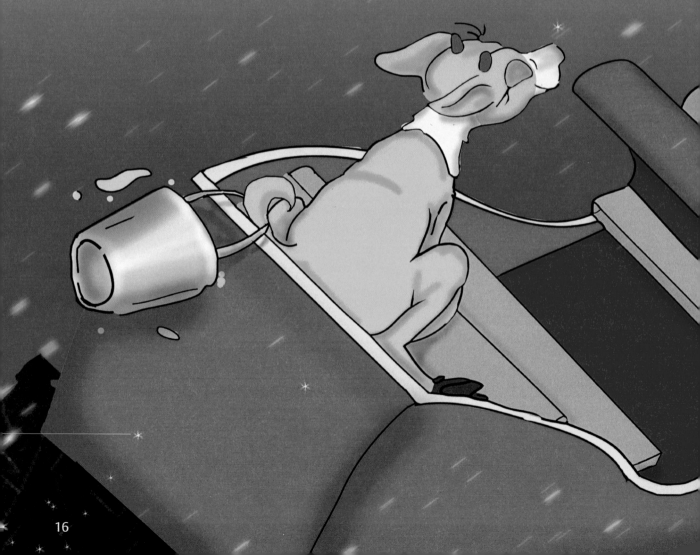

In fact, they built Darling a platform at the back of the sleigh so that she could go with them when they flew high in the sky above the North Pole while getting ready for Christmas Eve.

Then a few days before Christmas, Santa called a meeting of all the reindeer. He was happy that the children all over the world had been so good that the sleigh would be carrying more gifts than usual. But he was concerned that the weight of the sleigh could be a problem. Santa was worried.

There were more and more planes flying every year, and the sleigh would be heavier, so Santa and the reindeer wouldn't be able to fly as high in the sky.

"Will the planes be able to see us?" Santa asked. The reindeer became worried as well because they knew that they would have to fly much harder to pull the weight of the sleigh. They wouldn't be able to watch for the planes.

Right at that moment, little Darling trotted up
with her pail full of water for her uncles who had
been practicing their flying all day. As the pail hung
from the curl in her tail, it glistened in the brightly
shining sun, flashing a big bright light.

"Santa," Uncle Don said excitedly, "Darling already has a platform on the back of the sleigh because she goes with us when we are practicing."

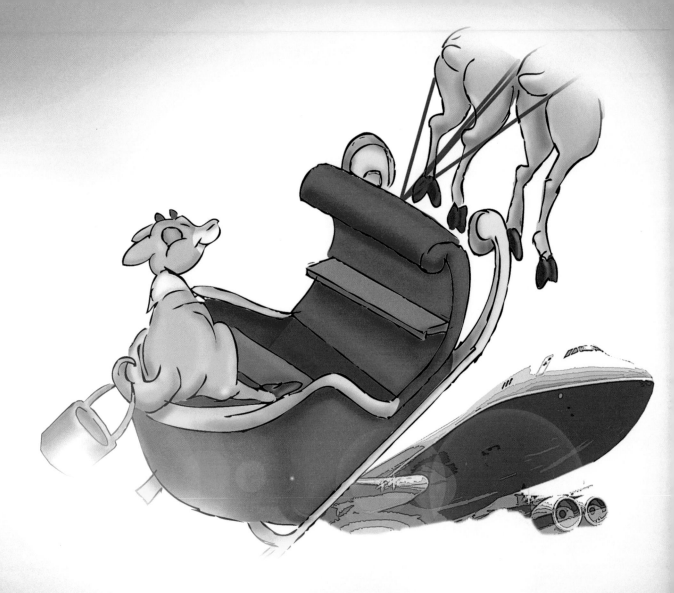

"What if we paint her pail so that it reflects the light from the moon, the stars, and even the airplanes? She can stand on the platform and the pail on her tail can be our light letting all of the planes in the sky see exactly where we are."

"What a wonderful idea!" Santa exclaimed. The elves immediately got to work turning Darling's pail into one that was shiny and bright. As a special extra touch, they sprinkled it with stardust that glistened like diamonds.

On Christmas Eve,
the moon and stars
were shining bright as
Darling climbed upon
her little platform with
the shiny, bright pail
hanging from the
curl in her tail.

As the sleigh took off and Santa shouted, "Ho, Ho, Ho," Darling looked at the North Pole below and took a very deep breath, "Oh my, because of the special curl in my tail, I get to help Santa on Christmas Eve to deliver toys to all the good little girls and boys."